Birthday
Book Club Donation
by

Mrs. Brusky

September 22, 2006

Birthday Book Club

© DEMCO, INC. 1990 PRINTED IN U.S.A.

THE RED WOLF

THE RED WOLF

Written and illustrated by
Margaret Shannon

HOUGHTON MIFFLIN COMPANY
BOSTON

für Ömchen

Thanks to Kate, Margaret Raymo, Tomas and
Ladka, Phil, Hooi-Ye, Linda White, and Roger and Putti,
for taking the pea out from under the mattresses.

www.houghtonmifflinbooks.com

The text of this book is set in 18-point Caslon Book.
The illustrations are watercolor, pastel, and colored pencil.

Library of Congress Cataloging-in-Publication Data

Shannon, Margaret, 1966–
The red wolf / written and illustrated by Margaret Shannon.
p. cm.
Summary: Roselupin, a princess locked in a tower by her overprotective
father, uses yarn to knit a red wolf suit to free herself.
ISBN 0-618-05544-4
[1. Fairy tales. 2. Princesses–Fiction. 3. Knitting–Fiction.] I. Title.
PZ8.S3365 Re 2001   [E]–dc21   00-056742

Printed in the United States of America
WOZ 10 9 8 7 6 5 4 3 2

THERE WAS ONCE a little princess called Roselupin, who was kept locked up at the top of a tall, stony tower.

"The world is a wild and dangerous place, Roselupin," her father, the king, would tell her. "Far too wild for my precious princess."

But every evening, as soon as the servants had dressed her for bed and locked the door behind them, Roselupin would climb up to her window and look longingly over the wild and dangerous world, until it was too dark to see it anymore.

So the days went by, all the same, until the morning of Roselupin's seventh birthday. On that morning, a large golden box was found outside the castle gate, with the words

FOR ROSELUPIN

spelled out in jewels on the lid. The strange box was carried up to Roselupin's tower, and everyone gathered around, all agog to see what was inside.

But when Roselupin opened the box, they saw that it was filled with balls of wool. Just different colored balls of wool, with a note on top. The note said:

KNIT WHAT YOU WANT.

The king roared with laughter. "Knit what you want!" he
crowed. "Some present! Tell you what, Roselupin, you can knit
me a nice scarf."

That night, Roselupin looked good and hard at the golden
box with her name on it. Then she went over to the box, took
out all the balls of red wool she could find, and began to knit.
She knitted and knitted the whole night through. And when she
had finished, Roselupin put on her new red wolf suit and said:

If the world's too wild for the likes of me,
Then a BIG RED WOLF I'd rather be.

No sooner were the words out of Roselupin's new red wolfy mouth, than she began to grow . . .

and grow . . .

and GROW...

until she burst right through the roof of the tall, stony tower and, with one giant leap, was out in the forest.

When the villagers looked out their windows and saw the huge, grinning wolf and the ruined stony tower, they ran to tell the king.

"My dear princess, eaten by a giant red wolf!" sobbed the king. "We'd better fill it up with food, before it eats the lot of us!"

So the villagers gathered up all the food in the castle and laid it down at the edge of the forest.

Ah, it was a grand thing to be a wolf! All day long Roselupin ate,

and danced her wolfy dance,

and howled her wolfy howl,

and at night she went to sleep peacefully under the stars, to dream of all the other big red wolves she had yet to meet and all the wolfy fun they'd have.

When she woke, she set off through the forest to look for
them. The strange thing was, the farther she walked, the taller
the trees seemed to be . . .

and the more she turned this way and that to find her way out,
the more the forest grew . . .

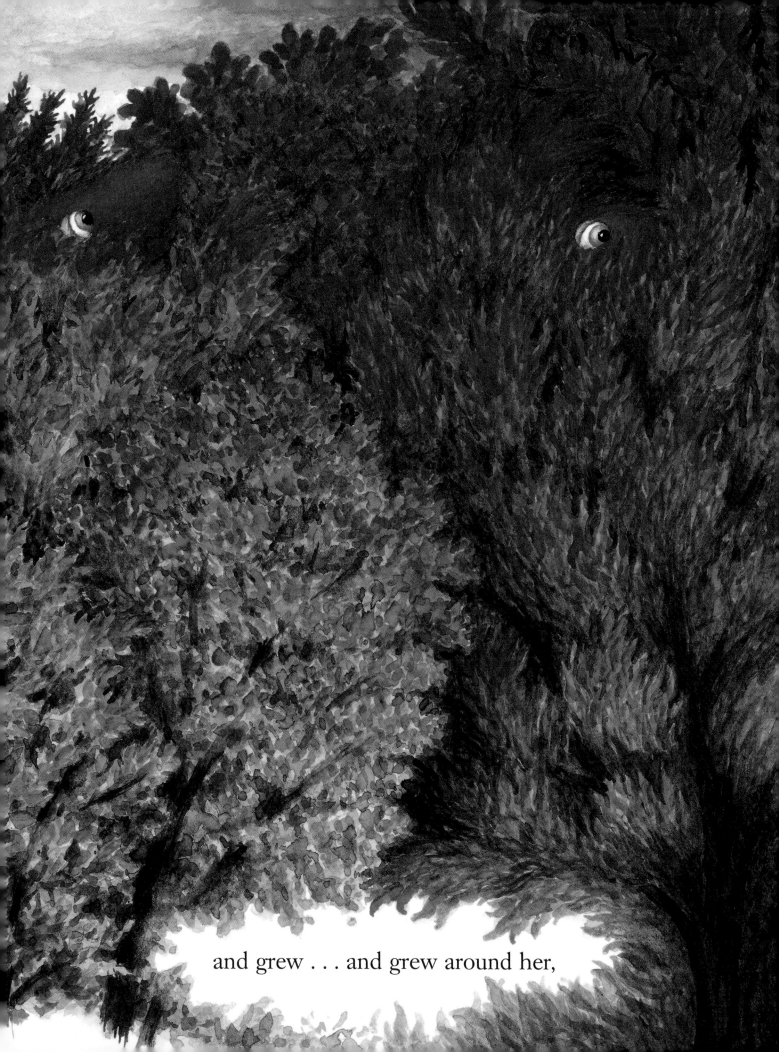

and grew . . . and grew around her,

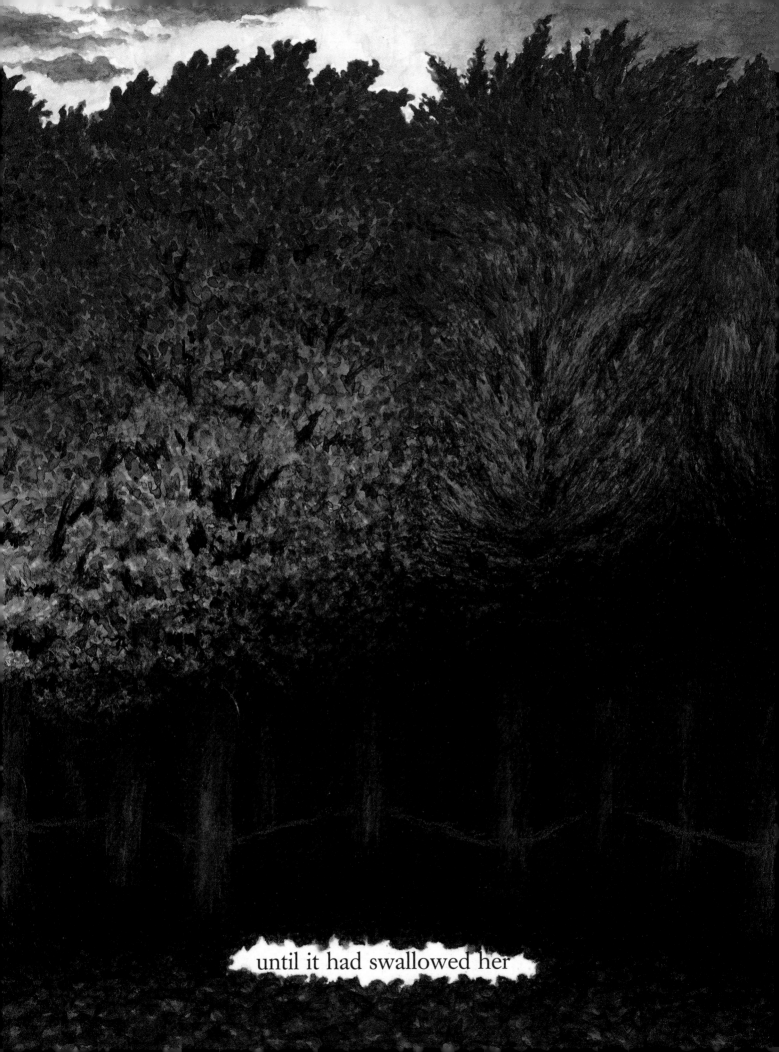

until it had swallowed her

whole.

When the villagers looked out their windows and saw that
the wolf was gone, they ran to tell the king.

"Hah! We must've stuffed that wolf so full of food, it popped!"
the king cheered hopefully. "I'll wear its teeth for a necklace!
Go and have a look for them."

The villagers looked everywhere, but they found no sign of the wolf. All they found was some red wool that wound and wound its way through the trees, deep into the forest,

to a small cave, where Princess Roselupin lay fast asleep.

They carried her back to the castle, cheering and singing, and told the king how the clever Princess Roselupin had escaped from the giant red wolf and laid a trail for them to follow.

"My little princess, still alive!" the king cried, clasping her tight.

And he ordered that a new tower be built at once, a tower even taller and stonier than the last—a tower no wolf could break through. There he locked her up good and tight, with a rich new gown to wear and the golden box of wool to keep her busy.

"Perhaps you could knit that nice scarf for me now, Roselupin," said the king.

That night, Roselupin looked good and hard at the golden
box with her name on it. Then she went over to the box,
took out all the balls of brown wool she could find, and began
to knit. She knitted and knitted the whole night through . . .

and in the morning, when the king came to see her, she said:

Please, father dear, be meek and mild,
And try these on for your only child.

Holding up, not a nice scarf . . .

but a rather mousy-looking pair of pajamas.